W9-AYR-685

DATE DUE			
AR 9 '94			
NY 3 '94			
MY 25 '94			
JE 15 '94			
JY 2 '94			
JY 29 '94			
AG 12 '94			
NY 9 '95			
JE 30 '95			

AN

SNAKES
and LIZARDS

A GOLDEN JUNIOR GUIDE™

SNAKES
and LIZARDS

By GEORGE S. FICHTER
Illustrated by DAVID MOONEY

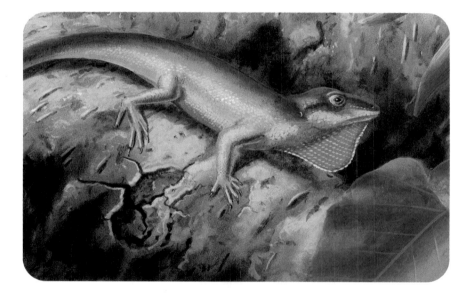

Consultant: Dr. Edmund D. Brodie, Jr., Professor and Chairman,
Biology Department, University of Texas at Arlington

A GOLDEN BOOK • NEW YORK
Western Publishing Company, Inc., Racine, Wisconsin 53404

752881

Snakes and Lizards

Snakes and Lizards are ancient animals. They are both reptiles. Modern reptiles first appeared on Earth more than 250 million years ago. All reptiles are *cold-blooded*. This means that their body temperature rises and falls with the temperature of their surroundings. They are most active when the weather is warm. On cool days, they become sluggish. In very hot or very cold weather, they hardly move at all. They crawl into burrows or under rocks and wait for the weather to change. In the following pages you will meet some of the most familiar or commonly seen snakes and lizards.

All Snakes and Lizards have plates, called *scales*, that overlap. A thin skin covers the scales.

snout

Rainbow Snake

tongue

nostril

head

scales

Did You Know?
Snakes and lizards are not slimy. Their scales and skin are dry.

Lizards are more common than snakes. There are about 3,000 different varieties. There are about 2,700 different varieties of snakes.

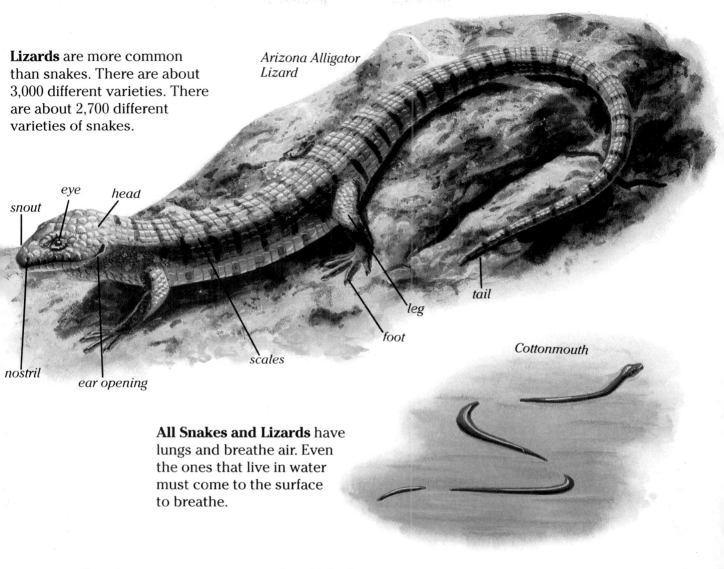

Arizona Alligator Lizard

snout

eye

head

nostril

ear opening

scales

leg

foot

tail

All Snakes and Lizards have lungs and breathe air. Even the ones that live in water must come to the surface to breathe.

Cottonmouth

smooth scales

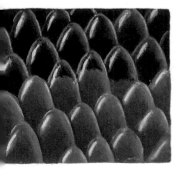

scales with keels

Some Snakes and Lizards have smooth scales. Others have ridges, called *keels*, in the center of their scales.

3

How Are Snakes and Lizards Different?

Snakes and lizards are alike in some ways, but there are many differences between them. Here are a few:

Snakes

- Snakes do not have legs.
- Snakes do not have openings for ears in their head.
- Snakes do not have true eyelids.
- Snakes can open their jaws very wide.
- Snakes have scales on their belly that are wider than the scales on their back or sides. In most snakes, the scales are in a single row.

Common Kingsnake

belly scales on Mud Snake

Prairie Kingsnake

A Snake wriggles out of its old, worn-out skin, revealing new skin underneath. The snake casts off, or *sheds*, its skin all in one piece. Some snakes do this twice a year. Others do it even more often.

Lizards

- ❑ Most lizards have four legs. (A few lizards, though, do not have any legs!)
- ❑ Most lizards have openings for ears in their head.
- ❑ Most lizards have true eyelids.
- ❑ Lizards cannot open their jaws as wide as snakes can.
- ❑ Lizards have scales on their belly, but these are never in a single row.

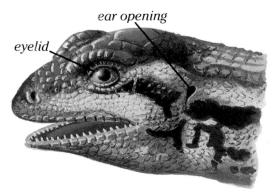

ear opening

eyelid

Sagebrush Lizard

*belly scales
on male
Eastern Fence Lizard*

A Lizard usually sheds its skin in pieces. Lizards shed their skin less often than snakes, about once or twice a year.

Prairie Racerunner

Did You Know?
Both snakes and lizards have teeth. They use these to hold on to their prey. A snake's teeth are curved. They look like tiny hooks. A lizard's teeth are straight.

Rattlesnakes

Rattlesnakes are the best-known poisonous snakes in the United States. There are more than a dozen different kinds. The largest is the Eastern Diamondback Rattlesnake, which may grow up to 8 feet long and wider around than a man's arm. The bulges at the rear of the snake's head are its poison glands. The holes, or *pits*, below each eye are sense organs that can pick up the smell of mice or birds from far away. They help the snake easily locate its prey, even in the dark.

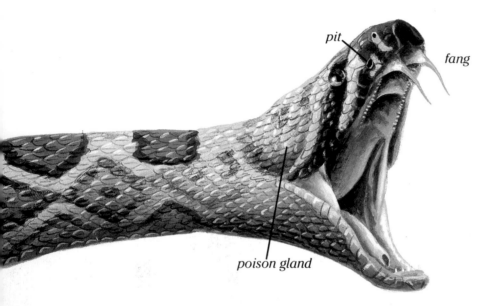

pit

fang

poison gland

A Rattlesnake's upper jaw contains two very large teeth. These teeth, called *fangs*, are sharp and hollow. They fold back when the mouth is closed. The snake uses its fangs to inject poison into its prey.

Did You Know?

Rattlesnakes are found only in the Western Hemisphere. The Sidewinder inhabits the western United States. Hornlike scales above its eyes give this snake its nickname of the Horned Rattler. The Sidewinder moves in a unique sideways motion over sand. It can go very fast.

6

Rattlesnakes have a special structure, called a *rattle,* at the end of their tail. This rattle has individual sections, called *buttons.* Each time the snake sheds its skin—and this happens several times a year—a new button is added. Older rattlesnakes have more buttons than younger rattlesnakes.

rattle of baby snake

rattle of young adult snake

button

rattle of older adult snake

The Rattlesnake's rattle makes a noise that sounds like dry leaves rustling. This is a warning signal to predators or other enemies.

Eastern Diamondback Rattlesnake

7

Cottonmouths are also called *Water Moccasins*. They live in swamps and along rivers and streams. A few may grow to 6 feet in length, but most are shorter than this. Cottonmouths spend a lot of their time in the water and eat mostly fish, frogs, and tadpoles. Like their relatives, the Rattlesnakes, they are poisonous. But Cottonmouths do not have rattles.

A Cottonmouth usually swims with its head and neck out of the water.

Cottonmouths

Did You Know?

Snakes, of course, don't
have legs. But they can still
get around easily on land. They
can also climb trees and swim.

A Cottonmouth that is
disturbed opens its mouth
wide. If you look inside, you
will see the cottony-white color
that gives the snake its name.

9

Copperheads

Copperheads live in dry, rocky areas and woods. They are named for the copper color of their head. Some Copperheads may grow to 4½ feet long, but few reach this length. All the *pit vipers*, which include the Copperheads, Cottonmouths, and Rattlesnakes, are poisonous. You can often identify them by their triangular-shaped head.

A Copperhead's colors and pattern make it hard to see among the dead leaves on the forest floor.

Northern Copperhead Snakes

Did You Also Know?
Mother snakes do not care
for their young. The babies—
rarely longer than an index
finger and usually narrower—
must find food and care for
themselves from the start.

Most Snakes lay eggs. Snake eggs
are tough and leathery. They are
not like birds' eggs, thin and easy
to break. But some snakes, such
as the Copperhead, give birth to
live young, often enclosed in
sacs. A baby snake cuts its way
out of its shell or sac with a
structure on the snout called an
egg tooth, which later falls off.

egg tooth

*babies emerging
from sacs*

Coral Snakes

Coral Snakes are poisonous, and their poison is very powerful. Fortunately, these pretty snakes are mild-tempered. They usually stay hidden among leaves or in loose soil. They might also be found under rocks or logs. Their fangs are short and do not fold back. Coral Snakes in the United States have red, black, and yellow rings around their body.

Did You Know?
Because a snake does not have true eyelids, it can't blink its eyes or shut them when it sleeps. However, the eyes are permanently covered with transparent, or see-through, scales. These protect them, like goggles.

Eastern Coral Snake

The Scarlet Kingsnake and the Scarlet Snake are both harmless. But they look a lot like the Eastern Coral Snake. Can you see any differences? For one thing, only the Eastern Coral Snake has a black snout. Also, the red bands on the Eastern Coral Snake are next to yellow bands. On the Scarlet Kingsnake and Scarlet Snake, the red bands are next to black bands.

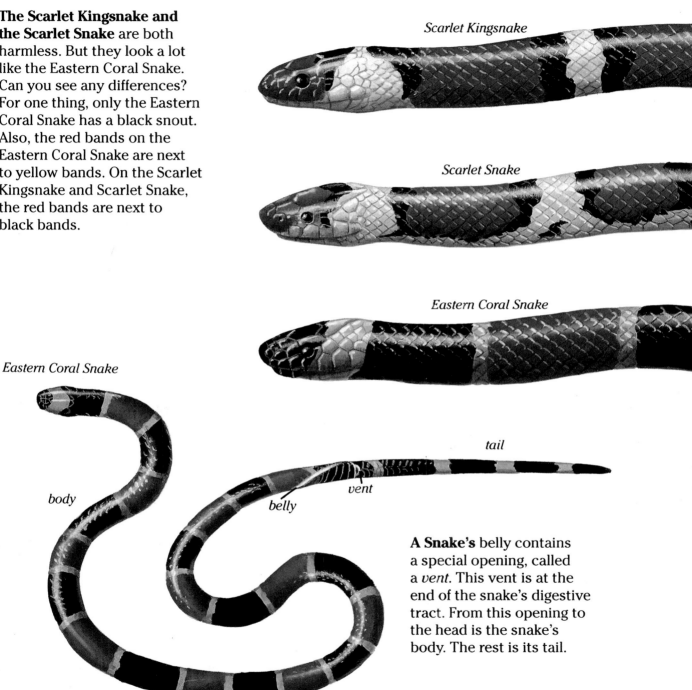

Scarlet Kingsnake

Scarlet Snake

Eastern Coral Snake

Eastern Coral Snake

body

belly

vent

tail

A Snake's belly contains a special opening, called a *vent*. This vent is at the end of the snake's digestive tract. From this opening to the head is the snake's body. The rest is its tail.

13

Garter Snakes are common throughout the United States. They are often seen on lawns and in gardens. There are more than a dozen different kinds. Most Garter Snakes are less than 4 feet long and have yellow or red stripes that run the full length of their body. Each of their scales has a keel, or ridge, down its center. Garter Snakes are generally peaceful and do well in zoos and specially designed reptile houses. They may give birth to more than 50 babies at a time.

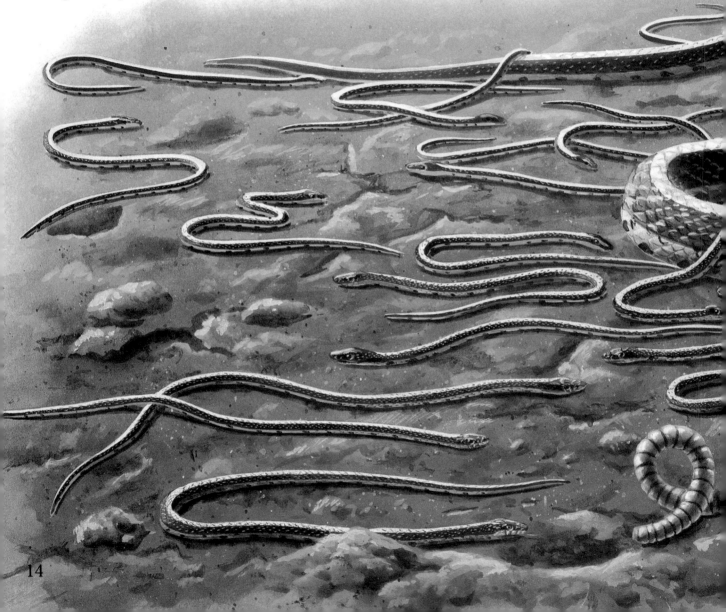

Did You Know?

When threatened, Garter Snakes give off a foul-smelling fluid that comes from glands in their tail.

adult Common Garter Snake with young

Garter Snakes often spend the winter together in an underground den. Sometimes, as many as 1,000 share the same home!

Most Garter Snakes eat earthworms, frogs, and other small animals.

15

Hognose Snakes are also known as *Puff Adders* or *Blow Vipers*. This is because, to make themselves look fierce, they can inflate their upper body with air and flatten their neck. But these gentle, thick-bodied snakes move slowly and are harmless. Their pointed snout, similar to a hog's, gives them their name. Most Hognose Snakes live in sandy areas. Some varieties are light-colored with dark blotches. Others are completely dark.

Eastern Hognose Snake

Did You Know?

Although they may inject a mild poison into prey, using the teeth in their upper jaw, these snakes rarely bite people and do well in captivity.

Eastern Hognose Snake (darker variety)

The Hognose Snake is a great bluffer. If it senses danger, it will lift up its head and begin hissing and swaying. Then it will pretend to strike.

Southern Hognose Snake

The Hognose will flop onto its back and let its tongue hang out as if it were dead, if bluffing doesn't scare away an enemy!

17

Rat Snakes

Rat Snakes kill by squeezing their prey until it dies from lack of air. A Rat Snake has a heavy body and may grow up to 7 feet, as long as a Rattlesnake. Its scales have small keels down the center. Like all snakes, the Rat Snake can open its jaws so wide, it can swallow an animal that is wider than its own body! Rat snakes are easily tamed and are sometimes kept as pets.

Rat Snakes attack mainly rats and other rodents. The snake swallows these whole.

Corn Snake

Rat Snakes can vary quite a lot in appearance. Some of the different varieties, shown on the right, are:

1. Corn Snake (brown variety)
2. Fox Snake
3. Black Rat Snake
4. Yellow Rat Snake

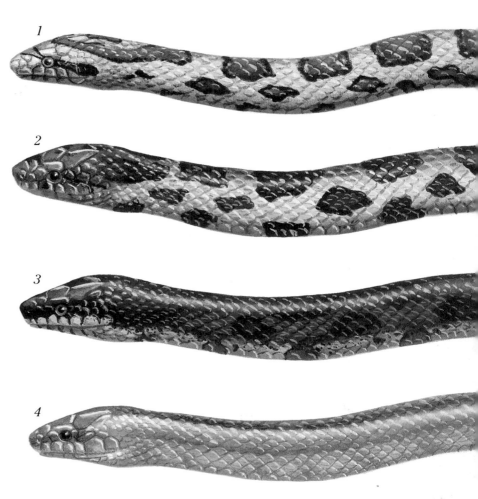

Young Rat Snakes have a spotted body.

young Black Rat Snake

Did You Know?
A few days before a snake sheds its skin, its eyes become cloudy. The snake is almost blind during this period.

Racers are slim and fast. They often slither along with their head and neck lifted off the ground as they search for a meal. But all snakes look as if they are going much faster than they really are. A person can run a lot faster than a snake can move. Racers like to eat mice, frogs, birds, lizards, insects, and other snakes. In fact, they will eat almost anything that moves and can be caught!

Northern Black Racer

A Snake's belly has broad scales. These help the snake slowly pull its body along.

broad scales

A Snake that wants to go fast moves in S-shaped curves.

Racers are nervous snakes. They are quick to strike. Although their bite is not poisonous, their hooklike teeth can tear the skin, causing blood to flow.

21

Water Snakes live in or near ponds, lakes, and streams. Their diet consists mainly of fish, frogs, and other small aquatic animals. Water Snakes have bad tempers. If they feel threatened they may bite, but their bite is not poisonous. When chased on land they will usually head for water. Most other snakes prefer to make their escape on land.

Northern Water Snakes

Like Garter Snakes, Water Snakes give birth to live young. They can have as many as 100 babies at a time!

All Snakes can swim, but Water Snakes can stay underwater longer than other snakes can.

23

Green Anole Lizards

Green Anole Lizards live in the southern United States. Like true chameleons, found in Africa and Asia, they can change color. They can go from green to brown and back again. This allows them to blend in with their environment and avoid being spotted by enemies.

Green Anole females lay a single egg every two weeks throughout the summer.

female Green Anole (brown form)

male Green Anole

A Green Anole male, when it finds a suitable place to live, blows up a red patch of skin under its chin. Then it bobs its body up and down to attract a mate. This also warns away other males.

throat patch

A Green Anole's body is about 3 inches long. Its tail may be almost twice as long as this.

female Green Anole

Horned Lizards

are also sometimes called *Horned Toads*. There are more than a dozen different kinds. The Horned Lizard looks a lot like a toad. But a Horned Lizard has a tail (toads do not), and its body is covered with scales (toads have warts). These unusual lizards wear a crown of horns, or spikes, at the back of their head. The horns protect them from being eaten by birds or other enemies.

Most Horned Lizards like to eat ants. But they will eat any insect or other small animal that comes close enough for them to grab.

26

Texas Horned Lizards

A Horned Lizard, to escape from the hot sun during the day, may bury itself in the sand. At night, it may bury itself to keep warm.

A Horned Lizard that is frightened or disturbed opens its mouth and hisses. It jumps toward whatever is close by. Most amazing, it may then squirt blood from its eyes!

horns in "crown"

blood from eye

Did You Know?
Horned Lizards are found only in the American Southwest and Mexico.

Fence Lizards

Fence Lizards belong to a large group called *Spiny Lizards*. Spiny Lizards have stiff, prickly "spines" on their scales. There are more than a dozen different kinds of Spiny Lizards. You might see any of them in fields or woods throughout the United States. They are good climbers and can run fast! Most are 9 to 10 inches long, including the tail. All are active during the day, when they hunt for food. At night they find a hiding place and rest.

Fence Lizards rarely come to the ground. They have sharp claws on their toes that help them climb trees. The wavy gray and black lines on their skin blend in with the bark. This makes it hard for enemies to spot them.

Did You Know?
A Fence Lizard has bright blue patches on the sides of its belly!

spines

Most Fence Lizards like to eat insects—especially beetles—and other small animals.

Eastern Fence Lizards

Did You Also Know?
Spiny Lizards have from 6 to 12 young. Some species lay eggs. Others give b.rth to live young.

Skinks are small lizards found on every continent except Antarctica. Their scales are smooth and shiny. Most Skinks are less than 10 inches long, and more than half of this length is their tail. Although they can climb, Skinks spend most of their time on the ground, where they can scoot along very quickly.

If a Skink is grabbed by an enemy, its tail breaks off! The tail keeps wriggling while the lizard itself escapes. A new, usually shorter, tail grows in to replace the one that was lost.

adult male Southeastern Five-lined Skink

Broadhead Skink

Did You Know?
Unlike most female lizards,
a female Skink stays with
her eggs until they hatch.

baby Southeastern
Five-lined Skink

Five-lined Skinks have five
yellowish lines running the
full length of their body.
Babies also have bright
blue tails. Older males
have a reddish head.

31

Gila Monsters

Gila Monsters live in the deserts of the American Southwest. They are the only poisonous lizards in the United States. Gila Monsters may grow up to 2 feet long, including their thick tail. They store extra fat in this tail and in their large body. The Gila Monster's raised, rounded scales look like small beads.

beadlike scales

Gila Monster

Gila Monsters like to eat birds' eggs and baby birds. They break the eggs and then lap up the liquid inside. They swallow solid food whole.

The Gila Monster does not move as fast as most other lizards. However, it has a swift bite and hangs on tightly to prey.

Gila Monsters do not have fangs. Poison flows into their mouth from glands in their lower jaw. It then comes out through grooves in their large teeth. Gila Monsters use their poison to kill prey and to protect themselves from predators.

tooth

groove

gland

lower jawbone

Glass Lizards

Glass Lizards are lizards without legs! Like other lizards, however, they have ear openings and true eyelids. They also have small scales on their belly. And, like some other lizards, their tail breaks off easily. Luckily, a new tail soon grows in to replace the missing one. Glass Lizards may grow up to 3½ feet long, including their long tail.

Western Slender Glass Lizard

Glass Lizards eat mainly insects such as crickets. They also like to eat spiders. They hunt for food early in the morning, when the grass is still wet with dew.

ear opening

eyelid

Did You Know?
The Glass Lizard, like the earthworm, lives in burrows it digs in soft earth.

Florida Worm Lizards are usually found only in northern Florida. Like Glass Lizards, they do not have legs. Their pinkish body is ringed, like an earthworm's. In fact, they look a lot like giant earthworms! Their tail is short and blunt. Using their pointed snout, they can easily burrow through the dirt, looking for insects to eat. These strange-looking lizards are blind. They spend nearly all of their time underground.

Florida Worm Lizard

tail

Florida Worm Lizards, after a heavy rain, will come to the surface to keep from drowning. A bird or person digging in the wet soil might uncover one that is coming up to breathe!

For Further Reading

With this book, you've only just begun to explore some exciting new worlds. Why not continue to learn about the creatures known as snakes and lizards? For example, you might want to browse through *Reptiles and Amphibians* and *Venomous Animals* (both *Golden Guides*), which contain many fascinating details on the animals in this book and additional ones as well. Another Golden Book you might enjoy is *I Wonder If Dragons Are Real and Other Neat Facts About Reptiles and Amphibians.* Also, be sure to visit your local library, where you will discover a variety of titles on the subject.